Jack and the Beanstalk
and
The Three Wishes

Retold by Rose Impey
Illustrated by Peter Bailey

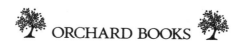
ORCHARD BOOKS

Jack and the Beanstalk

There was once a poor widow who had nothing in the world but a son called Jack and a cow called Milky-White. Jack was no help. He was a dreamer; he couldn't keep a job for two days together. But Milky-White was a good milking cow and saved them both from starving. However, the time came when the cow grew too old and her milk

Jack and the Beanstalk

and
The Three Wishes

For Siân
P.B.

Orchard Books
96 Leonard Street, London EC2A 4XD
Orchard Books Australia
Unit 31/56 O'Riordan Street, Alexandria, NSW 2015
The text was first published in Great Britain in the form
of a gift collection called *The Orchard Book of Fairy Tales*,
illustrated by Ian Beck, in 1992
This edition published in 2001
First paperback publication in 2002
Text © Rose Impey 1992
Illustrations © Peter Bailey 2001
The rights of Rose Impey to be identified as the author
and Peter Bailey to be identified as the illustrator have
been asserted by them in accordance with the
Copyright, Designs and Patents Act, 1988.
A CIP catalogue record for this book is available from the British Library
ISBN 1 84121 572 4 (hardback)
ISBN 1 84121 580 5 (paperback)
1 2 3 4 5 6 7 8 9 10 (hardback)
1 2 3 4 5 6 7 8 9 10 (paperback)
Printed in Great Britain

dried up. Then there was trouble.

"Now we're ruined," said the poor widow.

"I'll get a job, mother," said Jack.

"We've tried *that* before," said his mother. "No, there's nothing left but to sell the cow."

"Leave it to me," said Jack. "I'm just the lad to strike a bargain." And the same day he set off for market.

Well, Jack hadn't gone very far when he met a little old man, and couldn't he talk!

"Good morning, good morning and what a morning for a bargain. You look a smart lad," said he. "Where are you going with that fine cow?"

"To market," said Jack.

"I might be able to save you the trip," said the man.

This news pleased Jack; he was already feeling weary.

"And because I like the look of you and that *handsome* cow," said the little old man, "I'm going to give you such a bargain. What do you think of these?" And he held out his fist, opened his fingers, and there in his palm were five…beans.

"Beans?" said Jack.

"Beans!" said the man. "Not just one bean, not two beans, not even three nor four," said the man, "but five beans is the bargain and you won't get a better one."

"Five beans for my cow? You must think I'm daft," said Jack.

"These aren't any old beans," said the fast-talking man. "Believe me, these are magic beans. Plant them overnight and by morning they'll have grown into a beanstalk that'll make a hole in the sky."

Well, the word magic caught Jack's imagination. He took a closer look at the beans. They shimmered like a rainbow. They looked magic, all right.

"It's a deal," he said, and he pocketed the beans, handed over the cow and was home before his mother had finished her work.

"Back already?" she said, amazed. "I hope you got a good price."

"You'll never believe it, Mother," said Jack, bursting with excitement.

"Oh, Jack," she said with relief. "How much did you get? Ten pounds? Fifteen? Surely not twenty?"

"Better than that, Mother," said he. And he opened his hand with a flourish and showed her the five beans. His mother was speechless. But not for long.

"Beans!" she yelled. "Beans? You sold my pride and joy for a handful of beans? You idiot. You fool. You nincompoop!"

Jack's mother snatched the beans out of Jack's hand and threw them through the open door. "That's what I think of your precious beans. Up to bed with you. There'll be no supper tonight. Or any other night from now on." And she sat in the kitchen and wept with temper and hunger combined.

Jack climbed the stairs, a sad and hungry boy, but more sorry for his mother than his own empty stomach.

10

Next morning when Jack woke he wondered where on earth he was. The little window which usually let in the morning sun cast a green glow over the room, as if it were under the sea. Jack slipped out of bed and across to the window. Outside an enormous beanstalk twisted and twined its way into the sky, breaking through the clouds, its stalk as thick as the trunk of a full-grown tree.

Clearly, Jack had been right to
trust the beans, and he didn't hesitate
now. He reached out into the branches,
pulled himself up and disappeared
among the dense leaves.

Jack climbed and he climbed and
he climbed for most of the day until,
utterly exhausted, he reached the top
of the beanstalk. There was nothing in

sight but a wide, winding road. Jack walked along the road until at last he came to a huge great house, and at the door of the huge great house was a huge great woman.

"Good morning," said Jack, nice and polite. "I'm almost dead from hunger. Please, could you give me a mouthful of something?"

"It's a mouthful you want is it? It's a mouthful you'll *be* if my husband catches you," said the huge great woman. "He's an ogre. He eats boys like you on toast."

"I'll just have to take my chance," said Jack. "I'm dead anyway if I don't have something to eat. You wouldn't want that on your conscience, would you?" And Jack gave her the kind of smile that would charm any ogre's wife.

"Oh, all right," said she. "But be sharp. He could be back any time." She led Jack into the kitchen and gave him a bowl of porridge.

But as soon as he started to eat, the bowl, the table, the whole kitchen began to shake.

"Quick, here he comes now. Into the oven with you. And not a sound or it'll be toasted boy sandwich and no mistake."

Before he could object, the ogre's wife had bundled Jack into the oven, leaving the door open the tiniest crack.

The shuddering came closer and closer.

Thump! Thump! Thump! Thump!

Jack heard a voice like thunder
booming down the tunnel:

"Fee-fi-fo-fum,
I smell the blood of an Englishman.
Be he alive, or be he dead,
I'll grind his bones to make my bread."

The ogre thumped the table. "Where
is he, Wife?"

"There's no one here," said she.
"That's leftovers you can smell – last
night's stew. Come and eat your
breakfast."

Then she set in front of him a dozen
chickens piled high on a dish. The
hungry ogre ate, smacking his lips and
snapping and crunching the bones until
Jack thought he would faint from the
noise.

After he had eaten, the ogre took
out a bag of gold, emptied it on to the
table and counted it over and over
again. Jack peeped through
the crack and watched
the ogre. But mostly
he watched the
shining gold, and
thought of all the
things he and his
mother could
buy with it.

At last the ogre laid his head on the table and fell asleep, his snores rumbling round the room.

Then Jack lost no time in escaping. He slipped out of the oven, swung the sack of gold over his shoulder and set off for home. He ran as fast as he could, despite the great weight, until he reached the top of the beanstalk. Jack lowered himself into its branches and began to climb down.

When Jack's mother saw him safe
and sound she hugged him and kissed
him. Then, when she thought of the
worry he'd caused her, she scolded him
and smacked him. But when she saw
the sack of gold she hugged and kissed
him even harder.

"Oh, Jack,"
said she.

"Oh, Mother,"
said he, "give up."
Jack wasn't one for
kissing and cuddling. Still,
he was glad to see his mother happy.

For quite a long while Jack and his
mother lived well on the gold, but in
time it was gone. Isn't that always the
way with money?

So now they were poor again, and Jack wanted to go back up the beanstalk. His mother wouldn't hear of it, of course, but that didn't stop Jack.

One day, without a word, off he went, climbing his weary way to the top. He'd forgotten what a way it was, and when he reached the huge great house he was almost too tired to speak.

The same as last time, standing at the door, was the ogre's wife.

"Good morning," said Jack.

The huge great woman, being shortsighted, bent down and peered at Jack. "There was a young lad," said she, "looked remarkably like you, came here once before and stole my husband's gold."

"What a scoundrel," said Jack, looking as if butter wouldn't melt in his mouth. "I bet I know that lad. If you'd give me a bite to eat I could tell you a thing or two about him."

Well, the ogre's wife didn't know whether to believe Jack or not. But he had such a way with him that once more she found herself taking him in and giving him a bowl of porridge to eat.

Just as before, there came a shuddering and a juddering. All the plates rattled on the shelves.

"Quick," said the ogre's wife. And she bundled him into the oven again.

Not a moment too soon. In came the ogre. This time you should have heard him sniff! "Fee-fi-fo-fum," said he. "I can smell him, Wife, I can smell him."

"Surely it's only those lads you had last week and enjoyed so much. How the smell of boys does linger round the place," said his wife. "Sit down, your breakfast's ready for you."

So the ogre, still sniffing and snuffing, sat at the table and ate a pair of sheep.

When he was done he called to his wife, "Bring me the hen that lays the golden eggs."

As soon as it was on the table the ogre said, "Lay." And the hen laid a perfect golden egg. Again he said, "Lay." And it laid another, and another, each time he spoke, until there was quite a pile of them. Tiring of this, the ogre fell asleep with his head on the table, his snores like a gale howling through the house.

Jack had again watched everything through the crack in the oven door.

Now he crept out, tucked the hen under his arm, and set off at a run. He headed for the beanstalk and home before the ogre could wake and catch him.

This time Jack found his mother nearly frantic with worry

But he hugged her and kissed her and promised her anything if only she wouldn't be cross with him.

"Wait till you see this, Mother," said he. "Stand there, don't move, just watch. Now, hen," he said, "lay."

And the hen laid a perfect golden egg. And another and another, and she went on laying until the house was ankle deep in them.

Well, as you'll realise, this time the money didn't run out because if it did, Jack had only to say, "Lay," and there would always be more. But the truth is Jack had a longing to go back up the beanstalk, and nothing his poor mother said could persuade him out of it.

One morning, while she was still asleep, Jack set off again. When he reached the huge great house he knew better than to try his luck a third time. Instead he waited in the garden until the ogre's wife came out of the house.

Then he slipped in behind her back and hid, not in the oven, but in a large cooking pot over the stove.

It wasn't long before the ogre and his wife came into the kitchen. Thump! Thump! Thump! Thump!

"Fee-fi-fo-fum,

I smell the blood of an Englishman."

"I smell him, Wife, this time I *know* I smell him."

"Well, dear, if it's that rascal who stole your gold and the hen that lays the golden eggs, he's sure to be in the oven."

But when they looked in the oven, Jack wasn't there, nor anywhere else in the kitchen they thought to look.

At last his wife persuaded the ogre to have his meal and forget about boys.

The ogre reluctantly sat down, but he couldn't settle. Several times he got up and searched again. One time he even had his hand on the lid of the cooking pot. Jack stopped breathing and imagined himself sandwiched between two slices of toast.

But just then the ogre's wife came in. "Sit yourself down and tuck into this," said she. "This'll take your mind off troublesome boys."

She set in front of him half a horse. The ogre sat down, but still he muttered, "I could have sworn I smelt a boy."

When he had eaten, the ogre's wife brought him his magic harp.

"This is what you need," said she. "This'll calm you down."

No sooner was it on the table than the harp began to play all on its own. It played the most soothing and beautiful music Jack had ever heard. In no time, the ogre was lulled into such a deep sleep that his snores caused only the lightest breeze.

Jack carefully climbed out of the cooking pot and tiptoed over to the table. He was determined to have the harp for himself and his mother. But the moment he touched it the harp called out, "Master! Master!"

Jack didn't stop. He grabbed the harp and ran, as fast as he could, back towards the beanstalk. The ogre was soon behind him. Still dozy from sleep,

he stumbled several times and nearly fell
so that Jack reached the beanstalk and
was climbing down before the ogre
arrived at the top.

For a second the
ogre hesitated. Trust
his great weight to
a beanstalk, he
thought, not likely!
But again the harp
cried out, "Master!
Master!"

Then the ogre
began to follow
Jack, swinging
down the beanstalk
so that it swayed
from side to side.

When Jack dared to look up, he saw two huge great boots breaking through the clouds. That made him move even faster. As he slithered down towards the lowest branches he shouted, "Mother! Mother! Bring me an axe."

Jack's mother rushed out of the cottage carrying the axe. When *she* looked up and saw the ogre's huge great legs coming through the clouds she almost fainted. But Jack was down by now and seized the axe from her.

He chopped once, twice, clean through the beanstalk. For a moment it seemed to hang in the sky, then it crashed to the ground, bringing the ogre with it. He fell head first with such force that he was buried to the waist, legs in the air – stone dead. And that was the end of him.

So with more money than they could ever spend and the harp to always keep them happy, Jack and his mother had nothing left to wish for, except for Jack to marry, which in time he did. And then, since three can live as well as two, they all lived together and may still be doing so, for all I know.

The Three Wishes

One night a man and his wife were sitting before their fire, talking, cosy-like. She was a good wife and he was a good man so they were passing happy, most of the time. But now and again the pair of them couldn't help feeling just a bit envious of their neighbours, who were richer than them.

"It don't seem fair," said the wife.

"It certainly don't," said her husband.

"Now, if I had a wish," said she, "I know just what I'd do with it. Ooh, I'd be happier than all of 'em."

"And me," said the man. "Pity there isn't such a thing as a fairy, right here, this minute."

And suddenly there was, right there, that minute, in their own kitchen. All shining and smiling.

"You can have three wishes," the fairy told them, "but take care, once they're gone, that's it, there'll be no more." And then she disappeared. She was very business-like.

Well, the couple were amazed. They felt as if they had their heads on back to front.

"Whatever d'you make of that?" said he.

"I'll tell you what I make of it," said she. "I know fine well what I'll wish for – not that I'm wishing yet," she said, quick as a flash, in case the fairy was listening, "but, if I *were*, I should want to be handsome, rich and famous."

"Where's the use in that?" said he. "That won't stop you being sick and miserable or dying young. Far better be healthy and hopeful and live to be a hundred."

"And how would that help, if you were poor and hungry in the meantime?" said she. "Just prolonging the misery, in my opinion."

Well, her husband had to agree with that.

"Hmmm," said he. "This is going to need some thinking about. I reckon we'd best go to bed and sleep on it. We'll be wiser in the morning than the evening."

"True enough," said his wife.

But the fire was still burning brightly, so they sat on a little longer, talking things over cosy-like.

They were feeling that happy.

"It'd be a waste to leave this nice fire," said the man.

"It does seem a pity, though," said she, "we've nowt to cook on it. I wish we had a dozen sausages for our supper."

Uh-oh! No sooner said than done.

Down the chimney fell a long chain of sausages and landed at their feet. And that was one wish gone.

The man was flummoxed. He could hardly speak for rage.

"A dozen sausages! What a witless woman is my wife. Of all the harebrained individuals... I wish the dozen sausages were stuck on the end of your nose, you nincompoop."

Uh-oh! No sooner said than done.

The sausages leapt up on the end of the wife's nose and hung there like an elephant's trunk. And that was two wishes gone.

"Oh flipping heck, what have you done to me!" said she. She took hold of the sausages and tried to get them off. She pulled and pummelled them, she twisted and turned them, but they wouldn't budge. In sheer temper she jumped out of her chair, stepped on the end of them and almost tripped up. By now she was fizzing mad!

Her husband sat there open-mouthed, just watching.

"Don't just sit there gawping, you owl, do something, for goodness sake," she cried.

So then the husband tried too. He grabbed hold of the sausages and he pulled and he pulled. It was a regular tug-of-war. But the sausages just stretched longer and longer and longer. When he finally let go they sprang back like a piece of elastic, boxing his wife round the ears – biff! biff! biff! Then they hung down, long and floppy again.

"Oh, what a wretched woman I am," she began to cry. "Whatever will I do?" And her tears ran down the sausages.

"Don't fret," said he. "I know just what to do. We must use our last wish to make ourselves very rich. Then I shall have the smartest gold case in the world made for you to wear over the sausages. Maybe a matching crown. You'll look very grand."

"Are you a complete idiot?" said the wife. "Have you totally lost your senses? D'you suppose I want to spend the rest of my days trailing sausages on the end of my nose? You must have a screw loose. I want the last wish to get rid of these sausages," she said, "or...I shall throw myself out of the window."

And to show she meant it, she rushed across the room, threw open the window and jumped up on the window-sill.

Then her husband couldn't help but smile. The sight of his poor wife, standing on the window-sill with a string of sausages hanging from her nose, was such a comical sight. And, after all, they were still sitting downstairs, so she hardly had far to jump.

But he was a bit of a tease and he couldn't resist winding her up one last time.

"Of course, my dear, you must do whatever you think best, but it does seem a pity, knowing as how you wanted to be famous and all that. And truly, the more I look at it, the more it grows on me. I'm really beginning to think as it suits you."

"Suits me? A nose as long as a skipping rope? I should be tripping over it every way I turned," she cried.

"Happen you could wrap it round your neck, lovely, then it'd serve as a scarf an' all," he said, trying to be helpful.

At this, his wife was fit to explode, but the man couldn't keep it up a minute longer. He started to grin, so he got up and helped her off the ledge. For he did truly love her.

"I wish my wife could have her nose back to normal," he said.

Da daa! No sooner said than done.

The sausages fell on the floor and coiled themselves up like a pet snake.

"Well, some good's come of the bad," said she, "at least we still have the sausages."

"I'll build up the fire," said he.

"I'll put on the pan," said she.

"What a good idea," said he.

So that's what they did.

The pair of them sat late into the night, frying sausages and toasting their toes before the fire, and talking, cosy-like.

HANS CHRISTIAN ANDERSEN TALES
FROM ORCHARD BOOKS

RETOLD BY ANDREW MATTHEWS
ILLUSTRATED BY PETER BAILEY

☐ 1 **The Emperor's New Clothes and The Tinder Box**
    1 84121 663 1   £3.99

☐ 2 **The Little Matchgirl and The Wild Swans**
    1 84121 675 5   £3.99

☐ 3 **The Little Mermaid and The Princess and the Pea**
    1 84121 667 4   £3.99

☐ 4 **Thumbelina and The Tin Soldier**
    1 84121 671 2   £3.99

Orchard Fairy Tales are available from all good bookshops,
or can be ordered direct from the publisher:
Orchard Books, PO BOX 29, Douglas IM99 1BQ
Credit card orders please telephone 01624 836000
or fax 01624 837033
or e-mail: bookshop@enterprise.net for details.

To order please quote title, author and ISBN
and your full name and address.
Cheques and postal orders should be
made payable to 'Bookpost plc'.
Postage and packing is FREE within the UK
(overseas customers should add £1.00 per book).

Prices and availability are subject to change.